Otis

AND THE
THE Tornado

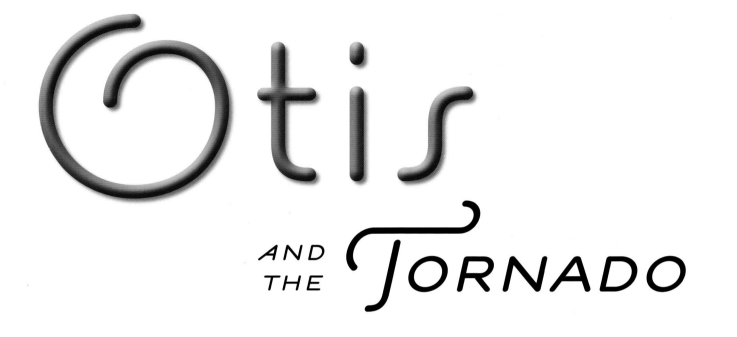

LOREN LONG

Otis

AND THE TORNADO

PHILOMEL BOOKS · AN IMPRINT OF PENGUIN GROUP (USA) INC.

PHILOMEL BOOKS

A division of Penguin Young Readers Group.
Published by The Penguin Group. Penguin Group (USA) Inc., 375 Hudson Street, New York, NY 10014, U.S.A.
Penguin Group (Canada), 90 Eglinton Avenue East, Suite 700, Toronto, Ontario M4P 2Y3, Canada (a division of Pearson Penguin Canada Inc.).
Penguin Books Ltd, 80 Strand, London WC2R 0RL, England.
Penguin Ireland, 25 St. Stephen's Green, Dublin 2, Ireland (a division of Penguin Books Ltd).
Penguin Group (Australia), 250 Camberwell Road, Camberwell, Victoria 3124, Australia (a division of Pearson Australia Group Pty Ltd).
Penguin Books India Pvt Ltd, 11 Community Centre, Panchsheel Park, New Delhi - 110 017, India.
Penguin Group (NZ), 67 Apollo Drive, Rosedale, Auckland 0632, New Zealand (a division of Pearson New Zealand Ltd).
Penguin Books (South Africa) (Pty) Ltd, 24 Sturdee Avenue, Rosebank, Johannesburg 2196, South Africa.
Penguin Books Ltd, Registered Offices: 80 Strand, London WC2R 0RL, England.

Edited by Michael Green. Design by Semadar Megged.
Text set in 15.5-point Engine. The art was created in gouache and pencil.

Library of Congress Cataloging-in-Publication Data
Long, Loren. Otis and the tornado / Loren Long. p. cm. Summary: When a tornado threatens the farm, Otis the tractor must try to save the animals, including the unfriendly bull. [1. Tractors—Fiction. 2. Domestic animals—Fiction. 3. Farm life—Fiction. 4. Tornadoes—Fiction.] I. Title.
PZ7.L8555Ou 2012 [E]—dc22 2010036770
ISBN 978-0-399-25477-2
1 3 5 7 9 10 8 6 4 2

To Chunk, we love you.

Life was calm on the farm where the friendly little tractor named Otis lived. It was summer. The sun shined bright, the birds chirped, and after all the work was done, Otis and his friend the little calf liked to play.

They would gather all their farm friends for a grand game of follow-the-leader. They would take turns being the leader as they marched along. Otis would go first, *putt puff puttedy chuff*, followed by the little calf, who would bound ahead, bawling all the while. Soon the horse would trot to the lead with a "Neigh, neigh," as his hooves *clip-clop-clip-clopped*.

Finally the ducks would waddle to the front with a chorus of "Quack quack, quack quack!" They all followed the leader...up by the apple tree, around the barn, down the rolling hill, past Mud Pond, beyond the cornfield, across the meadow, and along the banks of Mud Creek. What a fun crowd they were. Everyone was so friendly, except...

. . . the bull.

The bull was nobody's friend.
When he was not in his pen,
he was kept in a pasture
all by himself.

If any of the other farm animals got close, the bull would stand
at the fence and snort and snarl and huff hot air. Suddenly, with a
burst, he would run back and forth along the fence. Then he would

stop and glare at them, like a statue, never moving a muscle except to flare his nostrils. The bull did not like anyone. And everyone was afraid of him.

Once Otis tried to make friends with the bull. He took him a shiny red apple from the apple tree and invited him to play. But the bull snorted and snarled and glared at Otis. Then he stomped his hooves in the dirt and charged! The bull slammed into the fence just inches away from where Otis stood.

From that day on, Otis stayed clear of the bull altogether.

One day, the farm skies began to swirl and turn dark. The winds blew and the rain came down. The animals in the barn grew restless and jittery. The skies tumbled and turned, turned and tumbled. Otis didn't mind the rain, but there was something different about this storm that he could feel deep down in his pipes.

All at once the wind stopped blowing, not even a breeze, and the rain disappeared. The sky turned a strange shade of green and the farm fell completely still. The only sound Otis heard as he *putt puffed* toward the barn was the farmer shouting in the distance.

"It's coming fast, get down in the cellar!"

The farmer was in such a hurry that he had no time for the animals. What was all the fuss about? Otis wondered. Then he turned and saw something that rattled his frame and shook his fenders. . . .

A tornado.

And it was heading straight toward the farm! What would happen to all the animals locked in the barn? Otis sprung into action. He nudged the latch of the little calf's stall until the door swung open.

Next, Otis freed the pig and the sheep. The winds howled closer. He stretched to unlatch the horse's and the cow's doors at the same time. *Click, clack*, the animals were free!

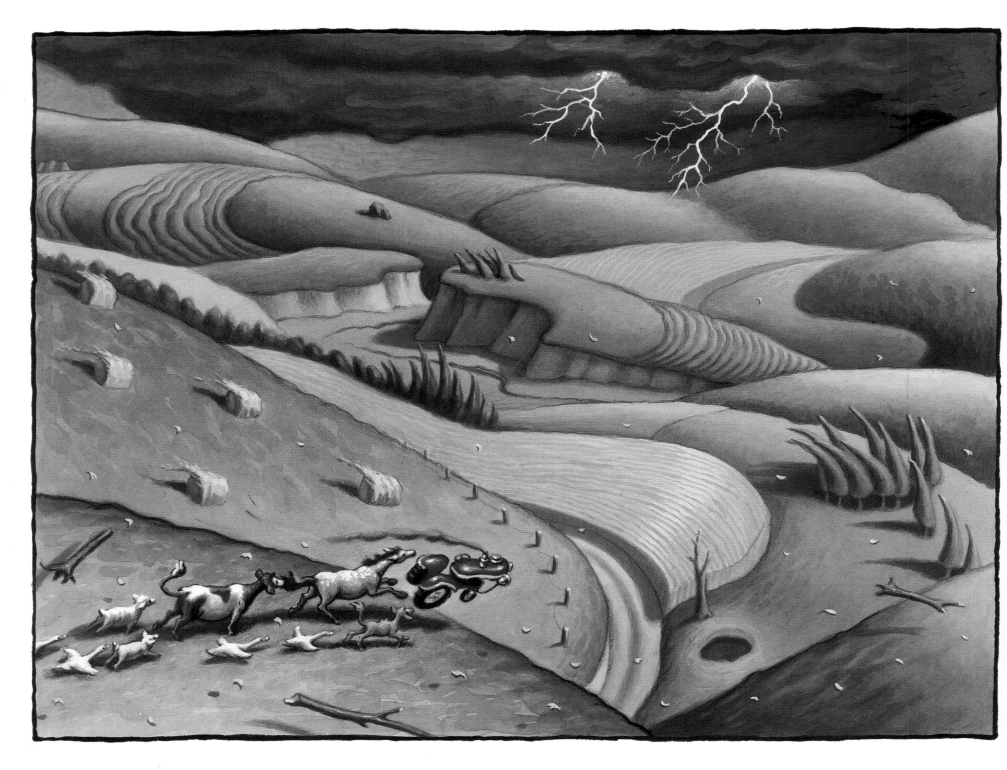

They followed Otis out of the barn and into the swirling winds. They followed him down the rolling hill, past Mud Pond, beyond the cornfield, across the meadow, over the bank, and down into Mud Creek.

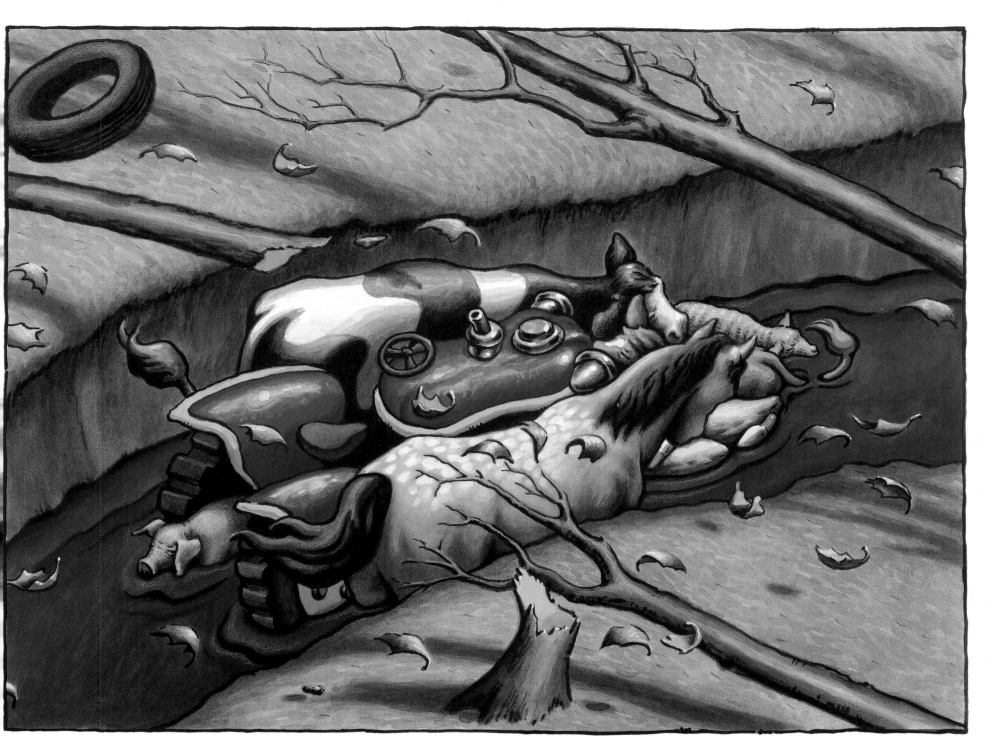

Tucked down at the lowest part of the farm, Otis, the little calf, and all
of their farm friends felt safe.

Otis sighed with relief. Now they just had to huddle together and wait it out.

But just as they squeezed close and tight, Otis heard an awful bellowing cry . . . the sound of a large creature in trouble.

The bull! He was locked in his pen.

From the safety of Mud Creek, Otis saw the tornado speeding in the terrified animal's direction.

Lightning crashed. The tornado howled. The bull screamed. And in a flash,
Otis was gone. He raced across the meadow, *putt puff puttedy chuff,*
beyond the cornfield, past Mud Pond, and up the rolling hill to the bullpen.

Otis found the bull tucked under the shed, shaking in fear.

Otis tried to unlatch the gate. It was locked. He slammed head on into it. The gate shook but held firm. Otis rammed it again. The gate teetered. The bull wailed like a baby.

Otis spun around, threw himself in reverse, revved his engine, and charged backward into the gate. *CRASH!* The gate shattered into pieces. Otis shook himself off, gave the bull a friendly *chuff,* and peeled out.

The bull followed Otis down the rolling hill, past Mud Pond, and beyond the cornfield. The tornado roared like a freight train as they crossed the meadow, and just as Otis and the bull dove for cover over the bank and into Mud Creek, the tornado touched down, narrowly missing them.

Otis, the little calf, the bull, and all
the farm friends ducked their heads
and closed their eyes. They'd never
heard such a fury or felt such a
rage, but they were all safely
tucked down in the muddy
creek's bed at the lowest
part of the farm. And
they stayed huddled
there until long
after the tornado
had passed.

They came out only when it was calm and
the sun shined bright and the birds began to chirp.
They found a farm that needed great repair.

Some afternoons we'd put on a show,
perhaps Peter Pan or Pinocchio.
There'd be costumes, tickets, and lemonade;
everything would be homemade.

When I was just a little girl,
my mother read to me
stories of fairies and ghosts
and pirates on the sea.
There were castles and knights,
dragons with wings,
Hansel and Gretel
and long ago kings.

When I was just a little girl,
my father took me to the zoo.
There were elephants and monkeys
and once a kangaroo.

My father taught me to whistle
and to fly a kite.
He always came in to kiss me good night.
He helped me learn my ABCs,
he held me close when I skinned my knees.

When I was just a little girl,
birthday cakes were just as sweet.

There were valentines and Easter eggs
and Halloween trick or treats.

When I was just a little girl,
Christmas was the best time of the year.
I loved the bells, the baking smells,
and Santa's eight tiny reindeer.

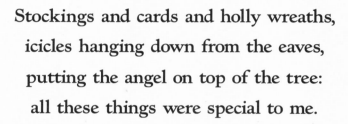

Stockings and cards and holly wreaths,
icicles hanging down from the eaves,
putting the angel on top of the tree:
all these things were special to me.

When I was just a little girl,
every night I'd climb the stairs.
I'd brush my teeth, crawl into bed,
and say my evening prayers.

When I was just a little girl,

sometimes I liked to be alone.

And I'd wonder how I'd feel

when I was grown.

Now I am grown, and it does seem strange
to think about how many things are still the same.
The sun is as warm, the stars are as bright,
I see the same moon in the sky at night.
And years from now when you're all grown,
that same moon will be shining on you.
And perhaps your children will want to know
just what you used to do.

And what will you say
if they want you to stay,
to talk to them for a while
and tell them about the things that you did,
when you were just a child?